The Fairy Story Book

By
Linda Williams
"The Manx Fairy Godmother"

Tales of the 'little people'
at Fairy Bridge Isle of Man

Copyright © 2012 Linda Williams
All rights reserved.

ISBN-13: 978-1479170265

To Frank, Steve and David.
Always supportive x

CONTENTS

Chapter 1   Cobba returns to Fairy Bridge

Chapter 2   Magenta and the Confetti Factory

Chapter 3   Flora welcomes us to Home-stay Hotel

Chapter 4   Jacquelina and sunflower seeds

Chapter 5   Bubs, Baby Bubs and Tud in their dinghy

Chapter 6   A Fairy Wedding

Chapter 7   Ghennal (Happy and Jolly)

Chapter 8   Christmas Feather Fairy

Chapter 9   Ben Varrey and Little Queenie

Chapter one

It became clearer as the Manannan Mist curled and lifted above the Foxglove Glen, that the day would, after all, be a good one. Balla sat under a dock leaf, waiting for his friend, Cronk. Balla was younger than Cronk by about six weeks. This is very important in status, when you are one of the 'little people', as they are known locally, on this fair Isle. They remember to give respect to their elders, and Balla always remembered that Cronk was his elder (by a mere few weeks), but it was enough for Cronk to be the leader, when it came to exploring, or setting up play for the day.

Cronk arrived, and had brought his little sister, Voirrey. This always added excitement and fun, despite her being a girl! Voirrey was very adventurous, and loved playing games. Spending time at Fairy Bridge, was a favourite of all to these little folk. If you have never been to the Isle of Man it cannot be said strong enough, everyone who goes over the Bridge, (in some cases, many times a day), will always raise their hand and say 'hello' to the fairies. Those who scoff, at such an idea, will find that some little thing will happen, maybe a flat tyre, or being late for an appointment, or lose something of value. Then they remember that they have forgotten to say 'hello fairies', when they last went over the Fairy Bridge. Voirrey as usual wanted to lead the pack, even though she was twelve months younger than Balla and Cronk. Her spirited nature added to her rather plain appearance, but everyone agreed that Voirrey, would go far, in whatever she wanted to do. Her hair was tied back with a length of cotton. She had found the cotton, around a twig, some time ago. Her dark hair was very unruly, and the curls escaped from the cotton tie, in defiance. Sitting on top of her head was a bluebell flower, that showed off the colour of her eyes. Her nose was rather long, for such a small face, and was covered in freckles. Her smile captured everyone. She would never be as beautiful as the Fairy Princess, but she would always be the centre of things, due to her sunny and friendly nature. Her dress was very plain, in contrast to her rather fetching headwear, and was patched in places, which gave the dress a rather unique style. Her feet were bare, as it was summer, and she liked to feel the grass under her feet, as she ran among the hedgerows. Her wings were as yet, small, but she could manage to fly for short amounts of time, and they would develop as she herself grew up.

By contrast, her brother Cronk, was very handsome, and smoothed his dark curls down with the juice from the rose-hips. His eyes were blue, and covered by long dark lashes, and twinkled when he smiled. His other features were perfect, and this gave him his overall good looks. He was not aware of this at all, and made many friends amongst the fairy folk, who knew, he would be a leader one day.

Balla was a different sort altogether. He lived completely on his own, despite his age, and was very capable, but had no care at all for his appearance. Nothing ever fitted properly, his hand-me-down shoes, always appeared, as if someone else was still in them! His clothes, although clean, never matched, and today was no exception. He had a cap on his head made from a seed-pod, to keep the sun from his blonde hair. His shirt was well worn, and a bit crumpled, and his trousers were made of a cord material, and they were shiny in places. He had a mischievous grin, and made friends very easily. This was his asset. He was able to spot a lonely fairy, and no sooner said than done, bring them into the spirit of the games with the others.

It did not take too long for Balla, Cronk and Voirrey to decide to go to Fairy Bridge. They lived not too far away, and the clear blue sky was beginning to show through from the clouds. The stream was very low, due to the good summer, and with little rainfall. Voirrey held on to her bluebell hat, as they ran down the slope, towards the Bridge. If someone came along they would take it in turns to peep, from behind a leaf, and to see if they were spotted or not. Sometimes, this little game went on for ages, as they would dart behind one leaf after another.

As they approached the Bridge, they saw another fairy. They knew everybody, but this fairy was someone new to them, and they approached with caution. They said hello, and were surprised when the fairy turned to them. His face was tanned, and they could tell that he was used to being out of doors. He introduced himself as Cobba, and he had an unusual story to tell. He said that his parents, many years before, had gone to live in Australia. They had hidden in the trunk belonging to some Manx folk, who had emigrated, to start a new life in Australia. Cobba said his parents had thought it was the right time for them to start a new life too. They had adventure in their souls. New ways and cultures appealed to them. They had many fairy children, and Cobba was the youngest. He had heard the stories on warm winter evenings, about his parents' lives in the Isle of Man, and how cold they had been in the winter time, but how beautiful the Island was. The glens, the beaches, the hillside, and he had decided, that he would like to return. He had managed to find someone who was also returning to the Island. He buried himself in the bottom of the large trunk, and it had taken many months to travel across many seas. Eventually, he had arrived in Douglas, and had walked for many

many miles to the Fairy Bridge. Along the way Cobba had been delighted with the beautiful countryside, and had met many other fairies. They had directed him, and gave him food for his journey. Some even knew his relatives, and he felt at home immediately. He was pleased to meet them too, and introduced himself to Balla, Cronk and Voirrey, in a strange voice. It was unusual to them. He explained that this was his Australian accent.

His parents had spoken in Manx Gaelic, so he was able to speak English and Manx.

   They were amazed at the stories Cobba told, and they sat until the early evening, talking to him. He said that he would be under the Bridge tomorrow, and they all readily agreed to meet him, and listen to more stories about his life in Australia. The three raced home, in time for tea, and told the other fairies of their encounter with Cobba.

So tomorrow, if you should pass the Fairy Bridge, and hear voices and laughter, you may have interrupted Cobba, telling Balla, Cronk and Voirrey his stories of life down under ! ! !

Chapter two

Magenta worked in the Confetti Factory, and she loved her work. Her job description was to jump into the boxes before they were sealed, and fill the box to the top. Magenta had to dress very simply, so that no dust or any contamination entered into the boxes. A few handfuls of lavender would go in, to keep the contents smelling nice. She always thought of the new Bride and Groom, and how excited they would be, starting their new life together. As a special gift from her, she always added a silver star or silver shoe or silver horseshoe and sprinkled it with fairy dust! Always look out when you see any confetti, the evidence that Magenta packed it, may be there for you to see.

There was soon to be a very special wedding. All the Fairy Kingdom would be attending. The Fairy Princess was to be married to her handsome prince, and Magenta had been chosen, for her special skills, and knowledge of confetti, to make up packets of confetti, for all the guests, including the Royalty. An honour indeed! She had been planning it for a long time, and knew of the colours, that the bride had chosen for her bridesmaids, and her bouquet. Every evening when Magenta went back to her little home at Lavender Hill, she would dry the flower heads that she intended to use for the 'wedding confetti'. Mr Quire and Mr Ream, the owners of the paper mill, allowed her to take any of the paper confetti, that had not passed inspection. It had very little wrong with it, but they were proud of their traditions. The factory had been in their families for many years. Every piece of confetti was checked by other fairy folk, and Magenta, was glad that she was not in this department! She preferred to be able to bounce up and down, like on a bouncy castle, all day. It was far too meticulous for her, to have to check each piece of the cut out confetti, but that is how 'Quire and Ream' had survived all the recessions and any take over bids, with their eye for detail and high standards. As Magenta had been collecting for sometime, her little storeroom, at the back of her mushroom home, was stacked almost to the top with the paper confetti. Thank goodness it was so light, otherwise Magenta would not be able to move it!

As usual the church bell tolling was

sufficient proof, that her time was finished for the day, and Magenta took off her little white slippers, and tucked them into her cupboard, neatly covering them with a small leaf, so that they would be nice and clean for her tomorrow, when she started again. She put on her sturdy leather boots. Her father had made them for her, as she had to walk home from the factory. The road was rather rough, and had holes in, where stones had once been, and so Magenta had to be very careful where she walked. Her friend Voirrey never wore any shoes, but she played in the fields all the time, and had no use for them. Magenta wore a magenta coloured dress always, so she returned home in her working dress, and would have another one ready, and all pressed and ironed, for her to wear the next day. She waved to her friends, who had also finished for the day, and set off on the rough road to her home at Lavender Hill. How lovely it was to smell the clean Manx air. She passed Syringa, gathering the fallen flowers from the Fuchsia bushes. Syringa was very clever, and, could transform these flowers into beautiful gowns, and, many little fairies wore them, to the many parties, particularly the Mid Summer Night Ball, and attended by everyone. The Manx Fuchsia was the favourite, but so many other varieties were available, in beautiful colours, it was hard to choose a gown. Some of the skirts had double petals and stood out like crinolines. Magenta had one for every occasion, and was known for her dress sense and unadorned ensembles.

   Magenta was thinking to herself as she walked along, and hoped the weather would be kind for the Fairy Princess. Her confetti would be in much demand, and if the sun shone, all the little silver items she had added, would glint in the sunshine. If it was windy, the confetti would lift up, off the ground, and would swirl around like a tornado, and the fairies would have to go indoors, as soon as possible. They could be swept away in high winds, and sometimes ended up far away from home. Then it would take days to walk back to their home again. It once happened to her mother and father, when they were young, and everyone had given up hope of their return. After many weeks, they arrived home, safe and well, with many stories to tell of the places they had visited, and other fairy folk they had met on the way. They reached Andreas, in the far north of the Island, and still kept in touch, with the fairies that helped them from afar.

  As Magenta turned the corner, she could see the Lavender Hill before her. She saw her friend Barrule, who had waited for her. Barrule was a lovely friend, and was also very beautiful. Barrule had long blonde hair, that was thick, and shone in the light. She brushed it 100 times every night, and it was her shining glory. As always she was immaculate, and wore a dark blue dress, with a little waistcoat, and it was embroidered with little three leg symbols. Her mother was very proud of her Manx heritage, and had taken many hours to embroider the waistcoat, and was delighted with the results. So much so, that she had requests to make others, and she was busy at the moment making some for the forthcoming wedding. Barrule wanted to go home with Magenta so that they could have tea together. Magenta was a very good cook, and was always gathering nuts and fruit when she could, and made delicious recipes, out of almost nothing at all. Tonight, Barrule knew, that some Manx Broth, and fresh bread had been made by Magenta, and she licked her lips, almost tasting it!

   Magenta opened her door, with the tiniest of keys, and let Barrule enter into her house. It was always very tidy, and (apart from the storeroom, that you opened with great apprehension, in case all the confetti blew out) everywhere was in immaculate order. Magenta made a drink of fresh blackberries and handed one to her friend in a cup made from an acorn. She would soon add some dry sticks to her fire, and put on the pot of broth, and toast the bread on a large fork, made from a bodkin needle. Your hands would not be burned, as you could stand far back from the flame, and turn the bread, so that it did not become too burnt! How many times had that happened? As busy human folk, I am sure you know how easy it is to burn the toast!

At last, after a feast, and another blackberry drink, Magenta and Barrule, sat outside, watching the sun set on another day. They had decided that they would not make up any more confetti packs tonight, but enjoy themselves, sitting outside, in the warm evening air. Tomorrow, they would start, as it would not be too long to the wedding day, and everyone had to be prepared for that.

Would you like to have an invitation

to a Fairy Wedding? Do you know someone as clever as Syringa, who can sew? Remember to look out for the confetti, especially if you see any silver stars, that may be on the roadside. It may have come from the Fairy Princess' wedding. Who knows?

Chapter three

Flora was a wise fairy, and could remember long, long ago when many fairies had to leave their beautiful Ellan Vannin, to find work. Many went to far away places, all around the world, and took their skills with them. They settled in America, Canada, South Africa, Australia, and New Zealand. In fact everywhere! If you go anywhere in the world today, and ask if they know a Manx family, you will be sure that somewhere near, a Kelly, Qualtrough, Kissack, or Corlett will be found, settled in their new Country. They will always have thoughts of their homeland. Do you know someone with a Manx name? There are many other names like Bridson, Bell, Brew, Callow, Cain, Callister, to name just a few. Have a look at the Manx Telephone Directory, if you visit, and see how many Manx names you can find.

Flora too had family far away, and could remember a great uncle who had emigrated to Cleveland, Ohio, in the United States of America to live. He had never returned, but as time went by, his grand children, and great grand children, wanted to come back to the Isle of Man, to trace their history. Flora had a large house by fairy folk standards, and had started the "Home-stay Hotel", so that visiting fairies had somewhere to call home, during their visit. They would sit with Flora, on her garden porch, in the evening, and recall, how they had met up with relatives all around the Island. The Manx language was still spoken, but these visiting relatives, could not understand it.

Flora used a gift tag to book in all her visitors. Her pencil, had been far more difficult to obtain, but one day, she found one by the roadside, at Fairy Bridge. Flora had, with assistance, dragged this huge pencil back to "Home-stay Hotel". Heliotrope, a very clever fairy indeed, cut, and filed the pencil, until it was just right for Flora to use. Not all the fairies were able to read or write, but Flora had been educated, and she passed these skills on to other young fairies. The hotel was used during the winter months as a private school, and most of the fairies came from far and wide to be educated at Flora's school.

Today she had many visitors arriving, and could not spend any time dreaming. If only her magic skills enabled her to wave a wand to complete the tasks, it would be wonderful. But many of these magical skills were held by the Fairy Princess and the royalty, and not to Flora, so she knew that start she must, on making the beds, and cleaning the rooms, that would soon be filled with her visitors.

The visitors were making special journeys, as it was soon to be the Manx National Day – Tynwald Day, held at Tynwald Hill at St Johns. The Manx Parliament is the oldest in the world, and not only fairies come to this event, but many ordinary humans too! A large fair is held after the ceremony, on the Hill, and the laws of the Island are read out in both Manx and English, and flags are waved. Schoolchildren have this day off, and with their parents they go for the day to see this marvellous ceremony. All the Fairy Kingdom, also visit, but they have to be very careful and hide amongst the large grass, so as not to be seen, by the human folk.

   Flora relied on Heliotrope to help her with the bed making, and they brought in fresh flowers from the garden. Freshly picked leaves would cover the beds, and the rooms would look very fresh, with the gingham curtains at the windows. A meal would have to be prepared too, as fairy folk would always be hungry, after their long journeys. Flora decided that her home made dandelion and burdock drink, always went down very well for the thirsty travelers, and Heliotrope rushed off again outside to find the ingredients, and Flora managed to lift the huge pot from the cupboard, and set it on the hob. She filled the drawer, under the hob, with some fresh twigs, set it alight, and in a few minutes, the pot was bubbling with the water, and other secret ingredients, together with the dandelion heads that Heliotrope had gathered. It smelt good indeed. Everyone around knew when Flora had guests arriving! Wonderful aromas drifted out over the glen, and everyone would try to call in, as soon as they could, so that Flora would ask them to sample the recipes she had chosen! Today was no exception, and Flora soon had several fairy friends ringing on the small bell at her door, to see if she needed anything for the new arrivals - and - by the way, to sample any of the little jam tarts, dandelion and burdock lemonade, or her homemade bread! She would always manage to bake more than necessary, and they would leave with a little parcel of homemade jam, scones or pastries. If you ever smell homemade bread baking, and cannot understand where the smell is coming from, you may be passing "Home-stay Hotel", and Flora will be busy, in her preparations for visitors. Do you have visitors staying with you? I am sure that in your home, many delicious meals are made, when you have people staying.

   Now Flora was almost complete, her tasks done, and all she had to do was await the arrivals. Some she knew already, as they had been before, but some were new to the Island, and needed a little map, to show them where to trace their family history. The Museum in Douglas had plenty of information, and was visited during the late evening. With luck, the Management at the Museum would leave some food and drink out for them. They knew what happened late at night! They had arrived in work many times, and found drawers open and paperwork in disarray. Now who could possibly have done that, after hours? They already had the answer – the fairy folk!

   Do you know anyone like Flora? Always baking and cooking delicious meals, but can always find time to ask you in, if you should call, to have a refreshing drink, or have a chat. These are true friends indeed, and if you know anyone like this, make sure you treasure them.

Chapter four

Jacquelina never had a minute to spare. She had a large family, and from time to time she had more people staying with her, than she had rooms or beds!! At these times every available chair or cushion was used, but all in all, they were all very welcome, and would not think of staying anywhere else, other than with Jacquelina. Even Flora, at the "Home-stay Hotel" could not entice them to stay with her!

Jacquelina was a very dainty person, with dark hair and beautiful dark eyes. She had a heart of gold, and would do anything for anyone. Loyal, sincere, and thoughtful would describe her, to perfection.

Jacquelina had a job at the garden centre, and knew all the different varieties of seeds by looking at them, and never mixed any together by mistake. She was able to grow almost everything, and the expression "green fingers" could certainly be used about her. Master Botany knew he had someone special in Jacquelina. Every year they would plant the seeds of vegetables, or flowers, and all the fairies would call in to hand pick the fruit, or dig up the vegetables. One carrot alone, would feed numerous fairy families for a week, so collecting was done on a rota system. Carrot soup with coriander was a favourite, so these were grown all the time. Mustard and cress could also be grown quickly, and the seeds were not too big to move. Fresh fruit, such as strawberries, and blackberries were a main part of the diet for a fairy, together with other seeds or berries found in the wild. Jacquelina made ice cream when she was able to supply the fresh ingredients. She placed it inside a little biscuit cup, and it was sold to customers at the garden centre. It did not take too long for everyone to know that ice cream was on the menu, and it sold out very quickly. Have you had ice cream made on the Isle of Man? Maybe they use the same recipe that Jacquelina has.

   Jacquelina knew it was interesting to see the seeds growing, and sometimes they grew so tall, it was impossible to do anything with them. These would be left to grow and grow, and the fairies would climb up, and see all around them, like being up in a tower. They could see for miles and miles. Once they grew some Sunflower seeds, that were so tall, the fairies could not even see to the tops of the flowers. They swayed from side to side in the wind, and they all hoped, the heads of the flowers would not fall down on them. At the end of the summer, when the flowers died, the amount of new seeds they found, kept them supplied for the whole of the next year. They know that sunflower seeds are very good for you.

   Sometimes, Jacquelina, would visit the Arboretum at St Johns, near to Tynwald Hill. This held many species of trees, that had been planted during the Millennium year, and now grew tall and strong. The only problem was, passing the ducks near to the entrance. They did not like the little people passing their territory, and made such a fuss flapping their wings, and shrieking for the fairies to go away. Sometimes a friendly mallard, would tell their family to stop shouting, and they would have a little chat with Jacquelina. She told them of any news from the garden centre. The ducks did not go very far, as they were well fed, with the visitors coming with bread etc., every day, and it was very useful, to let Jacquelina through, without fuss, and find out any news, or skeet as it is known on the Island. Occasionally, Jacquelina brought them some seeds. They found them very tasty, and it was a change from their bread diet.

   Jacquelina was due to have a holiday, and was hoping that the friendly blackbird, who came to visit the garden centre, would give her a ride across the water to see her family in England. It was a very long journey, but the blackbird was very patient, and was also grateful for the change of scenery himself. He liked to go across to England and he too could visit his family. Jacquelina travelled very light, so it did not make things too difficult with many heavy bags. Now, if the blackbird took the fairy from Onchan, she travelled as if she was leaving home forever! Her cases would have to be strapped together, and would fly behind, like a paper trail! But that is another story, and we will return to her later, if we have time.

Jacquelina went into the field, that also covered for the run-way, but could not see the blackbird anywhere. No doubt he was looking for food for his own family, and the farmer, not too far away, had his tractor out in his fields, ready for planting the grain. Jacquelina saw nobody, and so decided that she would go to visit a friend. As it was not too far away, Jacquelina used her wings to lift her into the air, and she moved very quickly and smoothly and rose above the long grass, and swiftly reached her friend's home at Foxglove Reach. It was a lovely sight to see the tall flowers, blowing gently, in the breeze. Bees were buzzing around, gathering the nectar inside the flowers. They then made it into honey. Jacquelina was very fond of honey, especially for her breakfast, and thought the bees were very clever to be able to create something so tasty.

The home of her friend, Fenella, was just at the edge of Foxglove Reach. The house had been created from a toadstool. It had a very unusual spotted roof, two small windows, and a tiny doorway, that failed to close properly.

Fenella had tried on several occasions to correct this, but eventually had given up, and left the door ajar. She had become fed up of trying to close it, the door was stubborn, and she had given up! This was her easy nature, and it showed as she greeted Jacquelina. She again gave the door a final push, to see if it would give way, but it did not! They laughed together, as this procedure had gone on for many years.

When they entered the toadstool, the room was completely round. Fenella had done well in finding many of the contents that she had adapted to fit into the round room. It was very cosy, and the sunlight was drifting through the windows, and gave the room a friendly glow. After their first hugs and kisses of welcome, Fenella went into the small kitchen to make a cool drink for them both, and wanted to know all the news. Jacquelina asked Fenella to look out for the blackbird, so that she could make the arrangements for her holiday, and they settled back in two large comfortable chairs, made from a walnut, with plenty of plump cushions, and had a long chat, before it was time for Jacquelina to leave, and return to her own home.

It is always nice to visit people isn't it? Do you go on a long journey to visit your friends, or do they live near to you, and perhaps you see them every day? Maybe you have a 'stop over' sometimes, and stay for the night. Do you know anyone who lives in a toadstool house, or somewhere unusual?

Chapter five

Bubs and his brother Baby Bubs were waiting for their cousin Tud. Tud was sauntering along the lane, whistling as he went. His two front teeth at the moment were missing, so whistling took great concentration, but he had mastered it, if he moved his lips to one side, which gave his face an odd expression, but he didn't care. Tud was the eldest of the cousins, and was tall, dark and handsome, even though his teeth were missing! Surely the tooth fairy could help him out, he thought. Never mind all those other little folk, who were waiting for the tooth fairy to call on them. He waved as he saw his two cousins, sitting on a small stone, watching for him. Bubs, was shorter in height, than his cousin, with blonde hair, and his eyes were different colours. In fairy folk terms, this is very lucky! He was as handsome as his cousin, but was as fair as Tud was dark. Baby Bubs, was very like Tud, although very much younger, and it would be several years, before he was allowed to have any say in what they were going to play, because after all he was only a BABY!!

   Today, as most days, their favourite game, was going out to the glen waterfall, in their home-made dinghy. Oh, the fun they had, and they would be out for most of the day. They always remembered, not to go out too far, as accidents can happen. Uncle Dobby always came with them anyway. He had been a boy scout, so he never forgot the safety first rules! Uncle Dobby would bring his newspaper with him, and sit in the sunshine, and read the articles. He did not need to read the paper, by the way, as he had printed it!! He was the Editor of the Fairy Gazette, and the newspapers, were printed twice weekly, and read throughout the fairy kingdom. Uncle Dobby now arrived, dressed in his shorts and shirt, and smart as always.

Baby Bubs, had been chatting away, and now smiled up at Uncle Dobby, and knew that he too would be able to go out in his own smaller dinghy. Whereas Bubs and Tud, would be able to go out unaided, except for a call from Uncle Dobby, if they went out too far, Baby Bubs, had to remain, by his uncle. Uncle Dobby, not wanting to spoil the fun for his nephew, had come up with an ingenious plan!!!

Before Uncle Dobby and Baby Bubs,

moved into the water, Uncle Dobby would produce from his pocket a long, long piece of string. This would be tied around Baby Bubs waist, and the other end would be looped around Uncle Dobby's wrist!! How clever he is. A quick tug on the string, and this would alert Uncle Dobby, if Baby Bubs had fallen in the water. He could swim, but not very far at his age, but he could enjoy the water, and Uncle Dobby gave him space, and would swim around, waiting for Baby Bubs to get bored, before they would go to the edge of the waterfall. Then Uncle Dobby would have time to read some more, and Baby Bubs would have a little nap. Then, as if by magic, the picnic would appear.

There were many fairies out today, and Bubs and Tud shouted to the other fairy folk, who were also in their homemade boats. There were all shapes and sizes of boats at the waterfall glen. They had been made from every sort of cap, or bottle top, as long as it would float, the fairies could use it! Every colour was to be seen, bobbing up and down on the water. They also had little paddles, ingeniously designed from plastic spoons, pieces of plastic, or wood, and some oars were even carved, by a proud parent, for their little fairy. Bubs and Tud, had two twigs, and they were very expert in using them. Their dinghy was quite deep in size, so water did not get in. It had been a cap on a bottle of some kind that the human folk had discarded. They had decorated it with some nail varnish they had found, and they had carefully swirled the brush around, so that the strokes looked like waves around the sides of the dinghy. Many of the other fairies, were envious, of their creation, and although they had tried, nothing compared to the dinghy that Bubs and Tud had designed.

Sometimes they would have a Regatta on the open sea, but only if the water was very calm. Then, every boat from around the Island would come, and it would take a great deal of planning to have this event. The adult fairies would have to organise it, but the little fairy folk, would have their own junior races to compete in.

This event only happened occasionally, as the Irish Sea, can be very choppy. The human folk, may be able to handle the rougher seas, but the little people had to take extra care, as they were so tiny. When the fairy folk spoke of a Regatta being held, it was very exciting.

Bubs and Tud were thinking that a drink of rose-hip juice would be very nice, (especially if Uncle Dobby had found some ice to put in), and to have a little cucumber sandwich, followed by an ice bun. They made their way, back to where Uncle Dobby was sitting, and he had already spread the little gingham cloth over a small stone slab, and the picnic was laid out, waiting for them. The ice found by Uncle Dobby, from under the waterfall, was beginning to melt, but they chipped a small piece from the icicle, and dropped it into the cup of rose-hip juice. Uncle Dobby had some ginger beer, and tucked into his cucumber sandwiches. They all sat looking out over the waterfall glen, and said how lucky they were to live in such a beautiful place as this.

Do you live in the country or by the

seaside? Maybe it is a place that everyone wants to visit? Or do you live on an Island like Bubs, Baby Bubs and Tud? No doubt sometimes, you wish that you lived in another place, because you think it more exciting. Well I guess, that other people think just like you do, and would like to live somewhere else. The most important thing is for you to be happy, wherever you live. Enjoy every minute you can, just as Bubs, Baby Bubs and Tud are doing. One day you will be like Uncle Dobby, passing on your skills to other young people, and look back on your childhood, and laugh at the funny things you did. Do you think Uncle Dobby will have a little snooze now, after his picnic? Listen out for his snores! zzz zzzz zzzz zzzz zzzz zz

Chapter six

The day dawned, and already the sun was warm, and the promise of a fine day, for the Fairy Wedding, looked very good.

The preparations had been in motion for quite some time. The ceremony, the catering, the banquet, all this had taken some planning. Have you ever been part of a wedding? How busy it is, but with good organisation it makes all the difference.

All the fairy folk had been invited to the Fairy Wedding, and this caused problems, of where to seat everyone, and would there be enough of the wedding breakfast, to go around!! Flora had been called in, and her skills in catering for large numbers. But, even this was a headache as it included hundreds of little people. She was on top of it all though, as she had many fairy helpers who said they would be proud to be part of this side of the ceremony. The meal was to be laid out "buffet style", and this would help enormously, and only require the helpers, to serve it up, as the fairy guests passed by the tables. Jacquelina was very good to help Flora, as well as a band of other fairy folk.

'Annie Go Lightly', who is another clever fairy, had been making parasols for the guests. This would protect them from the sunshine. She had collected the flower heads from the clematis, that grew around her. The variety Nellie Moser was her favourite, but she had mixed the different varieties, so that the colours of the parasols would all blend together. The Montana was vigorous in growth, so she was never short of a flower there! Comtesse de Bouchard sounded very chic, and these flower parasols were for the fairy royalty. Annie Go Lightly had called in Calluna, who lived among the heather. He was very adept at mounting the flower head, onto the parasol stick handles. Now their task was done, and they all stood proudly, the parasols sticking up from the ground, and ready for the arrival of the guests.

   Deutzia had been given the job of showing the guests to their allocated seats. Some were seated at the front, in special seats, made from runner beans. They were supported each end with a rounded piece of timber, making them into benches. Other fairy folk would have to stand, during the ceremony, but this made no difference to anyone. Just to be invited to this important wedding was enough, and it would be talked about for years to come.

   The Fairy Princess was becoming more nervous, as the time drew near, for her to leave her home, and travel to the open land above Fairy Glen, for her wedding to her Prince. Her gown was designed by Syringa, known as Lilac to her friends. The wedding dress was made of philadelphus flowers, and they had been sewn together with great care by Syringa, and her assistant Hypericum. The Prince, as a surprise, had asked the silk worms for enough silk, to entwine around her cape. The cape was made from a little organza bag. The Fairy Princess gasped when she

saw it, next to her bouquet.
The Fairy Princess, climbed into her carriage, that had been covered in rose petals. The two ladybirds, expert in the handling of carriages, stood proudly at the front, ready to go.

   All the guests were now assembled, and some were still tired from all the traveling. They had come from America, Canada, New Zealand, Australia, Spain, Italy, Scandinavia, England, Ireland, Scotland and Wales. In fact, anyone who was anyone in the fairy kingdom, were now seated or standing, waiting for the arrival of the Fairy Princess, and her father. The Prince was groomed to perfection, in his new suit, that Syringa had also made, in purple colours to compliment the philadelphus wedding gown.

The band began to play on their small horns, and drums, as the ceremony marched forward. How lovely everyone looked. All in their best Sunday clothes. Have you ever had to wear your best clothes for a special occasion? And, you couldn't wait until you could take them off, and be comfortable in something more casual? Well, all the fairy folk now felt the same, but it was on occasions such as this, that only your best "bib and tucker" would do.

   Soon the ceremony was over, and the Bride and Groom walked in front of their guests, and called upon everyone to join them for the wedding breakfast. How quickly they all moved now! All tiredness gone, only their stomachs were telling them how hungry they were. They all joined a queue, and as quickly as a hob- goblin could wink, the food was passed around. Plenty of tempting things were on platters made from shiny green leaves. The helpers moved amongst the guests. Beautiful fresh berries had been decorated. Their centers removed, mixed with crystallized ginger or honey, and then placed back inside the berry. The stalk from each berry had been left in place, and it all looked very appetizing. Nuts found in the woods, had been dipped in rose-hip syrup. Tiny button mushrooms had been mixed with the wild garlic, and all of this was the best cuisine on offer. Flora was congratulated. A toast, was given in her honour, by the Fairy Prince The sparkling water, had come from the Snaefell Mountain, and mixed with the nectar from several flowers. Many more glasses of this mixture would be drunk before the evening was over!!!

It grew dark, but still everyone was having a wonderful time. Little lanterns were lit, and the moon shone down on all the guests. Many were still dancing, and the band had played for hours, but they didn't mind. Occasionally someone would sing solo, or request for everyone to join in to a famous Manx fairy song. Everyone agreed that this would be a day to remember.

Did you hear any music recently carried by the wind? Did you see any coloured lights in the far distance, but not know where it was coming from? Or did you find some clumps of leaves on a large area of open space? This may have been where the Fairy Wedding was held.

Another day, you may look a little closer, at things you see in the countryside, and who knows, you may see one of the fairy folk at the Fairy Bridge yet!!

Chapter 7

   Ghennal, was mentioned to you, in chapter 4. Her name in Manx means happy or jolly. And, Ghennal was happy by name and happy by nature!! She was round in appearance, from her round face, to her round body, just like a ball with arms and legs!! She greeted everyone with great enthusiasm, and did the same with her work. Everything was a challenge to Ghennal, and she loved her little life completely. Her aim was to make everyone else feel happy, rather than to dwell on unhappy things. Think positive was her motto, and most times she succeeded.

   Ghennal lived with her husband Franzipan, who was a very patient man. Especially to have Ghennal as his wife!

But, they were very happy. They always had family calling to see them, or visitors from across the water, England, and beyond. Their family had originally come from England, and settled in Onchan, near to Douglas, the capital of the Isle of Man. Some of the family still lived in England. Some had gone long, long ago to Canada, New York in America, and Australia. Do you have relatives living far away? Maybe you have been lucky enough to go and visit them? Ghennal and Franzipan saved all their money so that they could travel on holidays to as many places as possible. Their Passports were becoming quite full with the authority stamps, as they passed through the various customs departments. You would not expect for the fairy folk, to have to go through such things would you? But, like you, they have to abide by the rules of the countries they visit, and so, fairy folk, have to go through 'Customs' when they travel abroad. Ghennal and Franzipan were quite used to all these procedures, and rather enjoyed it, as part of their holiday. Sometimes, on short journeys, the friendly blackbird would give them a ride on his back, but this was only for short flights. Most of their traveling included long journeys, and it would mean at least six suitcases! Can you imagine Franzipan carrying this luggage? Do you always have too many bags to go away? Ghennal wanted to be ready for any occasion, when away. If suddenly an invite to a fairy folk celebration, or a film premier, was given to her, Ghennal would have something special to wear! Ghennal wrote articles for Dobby, her brother, at the Fairy Gazette. A reporter pass, enabled her to "squeeze" herself into celebrity events, and write about it, and Dobby included these media interviews in a column in the paper. Any interesting "skeet" as Manx fairy folk would say, was to be found, in this column, and Ghennal, always had her nose to the ground, and her ears, to find out any forthcoming events.

Ghennal also had another brother, J.A. He was the local builder for the fairies. Occasionally, he had to build a mud wall, to prevent flooding, or repair a toadstool roof, it could be very difficult, unless you had the expertise to do it! All these were a challenge to him, and his band of fairy builders, were kept on their toes, as they were the only people capable of doing this work, around the Island. His two sons, Jo and Ja were on hand to help their father in this skilled work.

Today, Ghennal was making her way to the Fairy Airport, at Jurby. Not at Ronaldsway. where the human folk went to. It was in the north of the Island, and she was hoping for an interview with a very famous fairy. The large crowd gathered at the arrival gate, and they could not believe that the large basket, suspended from a colourful balloon, was now descending on to the tarmac, and it drifted down with some quick manipulation, from a member of the crew inside the basket. A large gasp of air escaped from the balloon, and before you could say 'Fairy Bridge', it was down to earth. There was a carpet of red, rose petals on the ground, and the famous fairy, descended, and was met by the Fairy Commissioners. Once inside the hallway, Ghennal found it almost impossible to scramble her way forward, to secure the exclusive interview she needed, for the Gazette. Her round and ample weight, worked for her in situations like this, and she used her elbows, that were surprisingly bony, considering her size, to great effect!!!! All those in front of her, fell to the sides, like a pack of cards, as she elbowed her way, to the front. Her hair was in disarray, but this was normal for her, as it was like wire wool, and sprang up all over her head. Although she tried to tame it, it was impossible to do anything with it, but on these occasions it would sprout up like a bush, and she tried frantically to comb down her hair, with her hand, before she met Ric O'Shea, the Irish leprechaun.

   He had met Ghennal on previous visits, and greeted her with great affection. He was dressed in a baize jacket, you would normally see this material covering snooker tables. It looked rather dashing on him. His trousers matched the jacket, and he had on a rather tall hat, similar to a top hat. This had a baize band around the rim, to finish off his dapper appearance. He was known for his quick fire jokes, and he 'shot' one at Ghennal to say how good she was to fight her way to the front. Any rugby star would be proud of her, he told her! Not very lady-like perhaps, but Ghennal didn't care, she had her scoop, as they say.

   Outside, Ghennal had a carriage waiting driven by the two ladybirds. They agreed to do it, on condition, that they had front seats for the first performance of Ric O'Shea, that was being held in the fairy style Gaiety Theatre. Ghennal now asked Ric O'Shea to sit back and enjoy his tour around the Island, before his stage appearance, and Ghennal asked him questions for her article in the paper. They visited Ramsey, Peel, Calf Sound, Laxey, Port Erin, Port St Mary and other beautiful places on the Island. Have you travelled on a coach around the Island? Maybe it was a mystery tour? There are so many places to see, it is impossible to decide where to visit first. Remember if you feel a little puff of wind, it may be a little fairy blowing you a kiss! Goodnight and God bless.

Chapter eight

The most important and prized call among fairy folk is an invitation to see the 'Elders'. The ultimate wish is to become the Christmas Fairy on the tree at Fairy Bridge. The Feather Fairy was delighted to accept when she was asked and she was very honoured.

Her feathery gown had been designed by Syringa. She had been commissioned to design the Fairy Princess's Wedding gown, and now had this task. You could not have any better than for her to design a special dress. The Feather Fairy was 'tickled' her gown was ready and it was suspended on a little hanger made from a cotton wool bud. It supported her gown very well and she twirled around the front and the back admiring all the handiwork that Syringa had put into it. The feathers had been dyed pink and lilac in a very large pot of special dye made from flowers. They were then hung out to dry on a fine dry day and the result was stunning. Have you ever seen a large amount of feathers swirling around? You may have interrupted Syringa at her work!

Even the birds the feathers had once adorned admired the results! Syringa and her band of fairy needle folk chased the feathers all over the place!

Once the feathers were caught they were put safely in the pot before they magically appeared for Syringa to sew together. As well as the dress Syringa had found a ring pull from a discarded drink can. She had asked the silk worms for a length of silk and wound this over and over around the ring pull to create a wonderful tiara for the Feather Fairy. Her wand had been made by the little Magician with a small piece of wire and covered with a gossamer material, and he had cast his magical spell over it so that if the Feather Fairy waved it, the wishes from the human folk would come true. To complete her outfit the eider ducks had donated all their discarded fluffy feathers to make her a cape so that when she was on the top of the Christmas tree she would not be cold. These feathers are used to make duvets for human folk so you must know how snug you feel when you go to bed!

   The Feather Fairy had been practicing for some weeks how to climb and also use her flying skills to reach the top of the very fine fir tree. It had been similar to learning how to climb hillsides with clamps and ropes! It was now a little easier as the whole tree had been decorated with baubles, tinsel, twinkling lights and of course angels' hair. The hair had been collected by the angels themselves from their hair- brushes and spun until it shone like gold. The Feather Fairy knew that she would be well looked after on the top of the tree by all the other fairy folk.

As the Feather Fairy climbed up the tree, she passed the little hob goblin who wanted to help her. His smile was quite grotesque but he was really very nice, full of mischief and it made her laugh at the things he did. He smiled at her now in his lopsided way and she gave him a curtsey as she moved higher and higher into the thick woody centre of the fir tree. Her parents watched from the ground, anxious to see that she did everything correct, but they didn't need to worry, she was 'impeccable' as they say, and would make them very proud. Have you ever appeared in a Christmas Pageant or a Nativity Play and saw your family in the audience? They smile at you but you cannot do anything. Well, the Feather Fairy now gave her parents a little wink as she reached the top of the tree and blew them a kiss! How proud they were. How beautiful she looked. Some of the fairy folk had travelled up the tree with her and now sprinkled her with fairy dust. It glimmered in the setting sunset. Once the lights were turned on, a glow surrounded her. She would carry out her duties with great pride for the fairy folk at Fairy Bridge. Perhaps you have never visited the Fairy Bridge on the Isle of Man. Some day you must call and say 'hello fairies' as you pass by. Local people would never pass by without saying hello, as it brings good luck. This is the place that visitors come to see as they have heard all the legends about the Fairy Bridge. To believe in your heritage is very important, no matter how trivial you may think it is. To keep these traditions, it is important for us to pass it on to our future generations. This is how the magic and enchantment of Fairy Bridge goes on.

   All the local human folk would now pass the giant Christmas Tree at the Bridge and look up to see the Feather Fairy glowing on the uppermost branch. Was she winking at them? Did they see her smile? Did they feel a little puff of wind? Or it may have been the Feather Fairy blowing a kiss! During the first evening, when the lights had been turned on, the local silver bands with Mr Crebbin and Mr Kneale had come to play carols. Everyone agreed how lovely the tree looked with all the baubles and things surrounding it. A special mention was given to the Feather Fairy. They could hardly see her because she was so high up but they knew she was there. The Feather Fairy hugged herself closer into her cape of eider duck feathers and was very pleased with herself. Sometime later the fairy folk would bring her a little food and drink to keep her nourished. She could shelter far inside the branches during the night time until dawn. Then she would be out again looking down, and all around, at the beautiful scenery of the Isle of Man. During the evening she could see lights twinkling far away in all directions. All the human folk now had trees adorned in their homes and gardens and all this added to the enchantment of Christmas. Christmas time is a magical time. But, always remember anyone who lives alone near to you. Surprise them with a special visit, make a hand made card or wrap up a few mince pies. You will be surprised how grateful they will be. It does not need to be something large for someone to appreciate. Remember they were young like you once. Perhaps they may tell you of their childhood Christmas times if you ask them. You may hear some very interesting stories. We often do at Fairy Bridge.

The hob goblin kindly stayed to watch over the Feather Fairy. He may look a little different but he has a heart of gold and will offer all his knowledge to the Feather Fairy during her special Christmas duty.

Would you like to be the Feather Fairy? Or do you think it would be very hard to do? Don't forget to call and see her and have a little closer look. Did she give you a wink? Or blow you a kiss? Or did you see a little smile on her face? This is the magic of Fairy Bridge and you will carry these memories for ever. Have a wonderful Christmas and look after those around you.

Chapter nine

Calf Sound nestles in the south of the Isle of Man. On a beautiful day you can cross over on a little boat and visit the Calf of Man. Many seals and basking sharks can be seen by the human folk as they sit having a picnic. Today, Ben Varrey the Manx mermaid sat on a rock and combed her hair. She was able to see her reflection today in the calm water beneath the rocks. Some days it was so rough she would swim far below to the bottom of the Irish Sea to escape the high tides and gusty winds that occasionally occur especially in the winter time. Ben Varrey means Mermaid in our language, this is rather nice don't you think? How would you like to be called Ben Varrey?

Ben Varrey had many friends both below the water depths and on land. The little people, or mooinjer veggey would always fly over to see her if they saw her on her little rock. The fairy folk were not too happy with the seaweed if it was on the rocks as it was rather slippery, but to Ben Varrey it was just another part of the sea and she delighted in it. Sometimes she made a headdress for herself from the brown seaweed. She had been taught many years ago how to do it. She twisted it around her nimble fingers and then had to weave the rest to create a crown. The seals were very impressed with this when she had completed it. They could swim better than her, but they had no techniques or ideas of how to make a headdress. Ben Varrey sometimes made one for them and they would balance it on their heads then toss it in the air to another little seal. This game made Ben Varrey laugh as they were so clever and agile in the water. Have you seen the seals at Calf Sound? Were they swimming together then diving under the water? Maybe they were playing with Ben Varrey?

Ben Varrey had long golden hair, and she combed it as often as she could. The salt in the sea made it very dry and it curled in ringlets sometimes. If she found any floating oil that had been tossed overboard from a passing ship, she took the opportunity to lift some into a scallop shell. Then she would find a sunny rock for herself and comb the oil into her hair. After a few hours she would then rinse it all away and her hair would shine like gold. She had found some small pieces of mirror. Long forgotten on the bottom of the creek and covered in small shells. She collected all these pieces and hid them in a cove. When she wished to comb her hair and see her reflection she would bring one on to a rock. She wondered if some day she may find another mermaid just like her. How unusual to have the head and body just like the fairy folk, (without wings of course) but instead of legs she had a long fish like tail. It made her swim like a fish, as the humans would say. The top of her body resembled a female. She was beautiful too and very unique with her fish tail

She sat on the rock that was a favourite and very comfortable. It was very warm today and her scaly tail glistened in the sunshine and she hummed an old sea shanty. Further out she could see Giant Dave, the Captain of the little boat, that took the human folk on their trips around the Calf of Man. He sometimes gave a wave to her but she wasn't sure if he could see her or not. Maybe he was giving a salute to the other vessels around the Bay? What do you think? As an old sea dog perhaps he could see Ben Varrey.

   All at once one of the little fairy folk appeared. She had flown over to see her. How clever they were to have little wings and be able to fly so easy over land and sea. Little Queenie greeted the mermaid with great affection. Queenies are the local word for scallops and as Little Queenie spent most of her time at the waters edge it was very suitable for her. She was such a tiny little fairy you could hardly see her. Ben Varrey had no problem in spotting her though. Her eyesight was very good. It had to be, so that she could sense danger in the waters as she swam around. Little Queenie was very excited today. She had something very important to tell. She snuggled in close to her little mermaid friend, even though she smelled very strongly of fish!

Little Queenie started her story. On one of her flying visits over the waters edge the day before, she thought she saw Ben Varrey sitting on one of the large rocks. Her hair was a different colour but Little Queenie thought it may have been one of the seaweed crowns that the mermaid liked to wear. On flying down a little closer she realised that this mermaid was indeed very different to Ben Varrey. She was very beautiful but her hair was definitely dark brown and her fish tail was rather smaller than Ben Varrey's. The little mermaid looked up and smiled at Little Queenie and motioned for her to come and join her on the rock. Little Queenie could hardly believe her luck to find her, and better still, to be able to tell her about Ben Varrey. The little mermaid was called Shrimp and wanted to know everything about the other mermaid. She had left home one day and had been caught in a large storm. She had tried to battle against the waves, but they were too strong for her. After many hours, when she thought she may never see land again, or a rock to rest on, she saw the lighthouse in the far north of the Isle of Man, at the Point of Ayre. After she had rested and fed herself from the small shellfish she found by the little whirl pool she decided to swim south. She did not know why but she felt as if someone was calling her, singing an old sea shanty and she followed the waves hoping to find a new home soon.

   Little Queenie was so delighted to tell her about Ben Varrey and said that as soon as she could the next day, she would meet her and take her to Ben Varrey. Now as the story tumbled out of

Little Queenie, Ben Varrey glanced by the side of the rock. She was shocked to see that someone had joined them by the rock, very similar in appearance to herself. They smiled at each other. Ben Varrey gave a warm Manx welcome to the newcomer and asked her to join them on the warm rock. Little Queenie was so pleased to have introduced the two mermaids to each other, and said she had to go urgently, this wasn't really true, but she wanted Ben Varrey and Shrimp to speak to each other. Oh what stories they each had to tell. The ideas they exchanged with one another.

This is what happens with friendship. You cannot do things always on your own, everyone needs a friend. Everything is much better when you can share the fun together. Little Queenie flew off to tell all her fairy friends. She knew that the little mermaids would never be lonely again.

Little Queenie is right isn't she? Do you have friends who you play with or live by you? They exchange their ideas with you. You will keep little secrets together too. Now Ben Varrey and Shrimp play together off the rocks, they laugh together and if you are very quiet and still you may see them both playing down by Calf Sound, if you visit the Isle of Man. Or better still, go in search of Giant Dave and ask him who he waves to at the Calf of Man.

The End

The Fairy Bridge Story Book

By
Linda Williams
"The Manx Fairy Godmother"

About the Author

Linda Williams was born in Liverpool, but has lived on the Isle of Man for nearly 40 years. She is married with two sons. She also writes poems and makes handmade gifts for her local Fairy Shop business.

For unique fairy gifts, please visit her online store
myworld.ebay.co.uk/mooinjerveggey

Mooinjer veggey means the 'little people'
in Manx Gaelic!

Made in the USA
San Bernardino, CA
04 December 2013